Barbie™ and the

MAGIC of PEGASUS

By Andrea Posner-Sanchez
Based on the original screenplay by Cliff Ruby & Elana Lesser
Illustrated by Carlotta Tormey

Special thanks to Vicki Jaeger, Monica Lopez, Rob Hudnut, Shelley Dvi-Vardhana,
Jesyca C. Durchin, Luke Carroll, Kelly Shin, Anita Lee, Sean Newton, Mike Douglas,
Dave Gagnon, Derek Goodfellow, Teresa Johnston, and Walter P. Martishius

 A GOLDEN BOOK • NEW YORK

Published in the United States by Golden Books, an imprint of Random House Children's Books,
a division of Random House, Inc., New York, and simultaneously in Canada by Random House
of Canada Limited, Toronto. No part of this book may be reproduced or copied in any form
without permission from the copyright owner. Golden Books, A Golden Book, and the G colophon
are registered trademarks of Random House, Inc.
Library of Congress Control Number: 2005922696   ISBN: 0-375-83340-4
www.goldenbooks.com
Printed in the United States of America   10 9 8 7 6 5 4 3 2 1

Many years ago, on the morning of her sixteenth birthday, Princess Annika sneaked out of the palace and went ice-skating on a frozen river. Annika loved having adventures, but her parents hardly ever let her do anything fun and exciting.

An adorable bear cub watched as the princess jumped up into the air and spun faster and faster. When Annika realized the cub was alone—and cold—she decided to take her home. "I think I'll call you Shiver," the princess told her new friend.

Annika hid Shiver inside her coat and went back to the castle. The King and Queen were relieved to see her. "We don't want you to wander from the castle again," said the King, "and there's only one way to make sure you don't—no more ice-skating."

"It's not fair!" shouted the princess as she ran to her room, crying.

Suddenly, Annika saw fireworks coming from the village below. She peeked out the window and saw people skating on a frozen pond.

"Shiver, what do you say we go to a party?" Annika asked.

The princess changed into a gorgeous gown. Then she sneaked outside—with her ice skates!

The villagers were thrilled to have the princess join them. As she started to skate, a dark, winged creature called a griffin landed on the ice. An evil wizard jumped off the griffin's back and walked around Annika, admiring her beauty.

"Allow me to introduce myself," the wizard said as he held out a ring to the princess. "I am Wenlock—your future husband."

Just then, the King and Queen rode up in the royal carriage.

"No! No!" shouted the King. "Leave her alone!"

"Don't you know by now that nobody tells me what to do?" replied Wenlock. "Maybe you've forgotten what happened to your other daughter."

Annika was puzzled. What other daughter?

Wenlock raised his magic wand and turned the King, the Queen, and all the villagers into stone!

"Marry me and I'll set them all free," the evil wizard told Annika. "Or you can join them."

Suddenly, a flying horse with a beautiful crown soared down from the sky. "Climb on," the horse said to Annika.

As the princess and Shiver flew away, Wenlock told Annika that she had just three days to change her mind.

"Marry me by then," he threatened, "or everyone will remain stone forever!"

Annika wanted to thank her rescuer, but she didn't know the horse's name.

"I am Brietta," the horse told her.

Brietta flew Annika and Shiver to a city in the sky called the Cloud Kingdom. It was amazing! Magnificent winged horses of every size and color flew all around them. Annika was taken to the palace and introduced to the beautiful Cloud Queen.

The Queen told her all about Brietta.

"She's my sister?" Annika gasped.

"Years ago, Wenlock wanted to marry Brietta," the Queen explained. "When she refused him, Wenlock turned her into a flying horse. The King and Queen desperately tried to break the spell, but it was too powerful. Brietta couldn't bear to see them so unhappy, so she left and came to live in the Cloud Kingdom."

Now Annika understood why her parents were always so worried about her. "I have to save them!" she cried.

"The only thing that is powerful enough to stop Wenlock is the Wand of Light," explained the Cloud Queen. "It is built from a Measure of Courage, a Ring of Love, and a Gem of Ice lit by Hope's Eternal Flame."

Brietta had tried to build the Wand of Light for years with no luck, but Annika convinced Brietta to try again—with her help.

Before Brietta and Annika left, the Cloud Queen placed a crystal bell around Brietta's neck. "If you need help, use this bell to call me," she said.

The three friends started their search in the Forbidden Forest. They didn't make it very far before getting into trouble. Shiver fell down an ice gully, and Annika and Brietta were caught in traps. As the sisters hung helplessly from a tree, a handsome young man named Aidan rode up on his horse. He used his sword to free them.

Shiver was still missing, so Annika leaped down into the ice gully. Aidan was impressed by Annika's bravery and spirit and decided to help her.

Annika slipped down the gully and landed in a giant's soup pot! She and Shiver had to escape before they were eaten! Annika decided to trick the giant. "There's a giant down the road much bigger than you," Annika said. "And he can tie himself to a post with a huge chain, lock it up, then break free with a single breath."

To prove he was just as strong, the giant tied himself up. Annika and Shiver quickly used Annika's hair ribbon to climb out of the soup pot, and they ran away before he could break free.

When they rejoined Brietta and Aidan, Annika explained how she and Shiver had escaped with her hair ribbon.

"The ribbon is your exact height," Brietta commented. "Your exact measure. A Measure of Courage!"

Magically, the ribbon sparkled. Then it turned into a glittering staff. It was the staff for the Wand of Light!

Next their quest to find the Gem of Ice led them to a snowy landscape. They searched for miles and miles but couldn't find anything. Exhausted, the adventurers built a shelter in a snowbank and settled down for the night.

The next morning, Annika, Brietta, Aidan, and Shiver were amazed by the beautiful sunrise. "What says hope more than dawn?" Annika asked, convinced that the sunrise must be Hope's Eternal Flame. Then she noticed that the sun was shining on a glacier. "The Gem of Ice is on top of that glacier. I can feel it."

Brietta flew the friends up to the crest of the glacier. Stepping-stones magically appeared, leading down to an icy wall covered with ancient writing. Aidan was able to read the words: *Beware. Take only what you need, but never from greed.*

As he read, the ground rumbled and a cavern was revealed. Shiver's eyes lit up as she saw hundreds of sparkling gems!

Annika pulled a perfect diamond from the wall. The ground quaked a bit. Then all was calm. Annika looked back and saw Shiver grabbing as many gems as her paws could hold. Suddenly, the glacier shook wildly, and ice cracked and fell all around them. Shiver dropped the beautiful gems, and the three friends quickly hopped onto Brietta's back. Then Brietta flew everyone out just before the cavern collapsed!

Once on safe ground, Annika held up the shiny staff and the diamond. "Now all we need is the Ring of Love," she said excitedly.

"Maybe I can make one," Aidan offered. He built a roaring fire and was about to melt his sword to make metal for the ring when Brietta offered her beautiful crown instead.

"But you'll never get it back," Annika told her sister.

"It's our kingdom and our parents," Brietta said. "I love them." With those words, the crown began to glow. Maybe the Ring of Love didn't have to be a ring for your finger, Annika thought.

Suddenly, a magic energy connected the diamond, the staff, and the gold crown! As the sun rose on the third and final day, the Wand of Light was finished. But would it work?

Annika lifted the wand and closed her eyes. "Wand of Light, I wish from the bottom of my heart to break Wenlock's spell over my sister."

Instantly, magic dust swirled around Brietta—she was a girl again! "Annika, thank you!" Brietta exclaimed.

Now they could defeat Wenlock. But they were miles from home and Brietta couldn't fly anymore! Just then, Brietta remembered the crystal bell around her neck.

"Cloud Queen, please send us some horses," she said as she gently rang the bell. Soon two winged horses swooped down from the sky.

Just as Annika and Brietta took off, the evil Wenlock flew up behind them! He fired his wand at Brietta, and she fell from her horse. Annika was so angry that she raised the Wand of Light toward the wizard.

"Destroy him!" she shouted. But the wand didn't work—and time was running out.

"Release my parents and the others, and I'll marry you," Annika said sadly.

"I don't want you anymore," replied Wenlock as he fired his wand by Annika's feet. The ground gave way, and Annika fell into the hole. Wenlock grabbed the Wand of Light and flew away to his palace.

Aidan and Brietta quickly dug through the snow to rescue the injured princess. Then the friends leaped onto the winged horses with Annika and flew to the Cloud Kingdom for help.

"Please wake up. I need you," Aidan whispered as he sat by the sleeping princess. Annika slowly woke up to find Aidan, Brietta, and the Cloud Queen looking at her. Her joy turned to panic when she realized that the sun was setting on the third day. Time was running out to save her parents and the kingdom!

Aidan and Annika sneaked into Wenlock's palace. Annika quickly found the Wand of Light, but Wenlock knocked it out of her hand.

The wizard ordered his trolls to retrieve it. That was when Annika noticed that each troll was wearing a wedding band. They were Wenlock's former wives!

"If I had the Wand of Light, I could make life better for everyone," Annika promised the trolls. Against Wenlock's orders, they tossed the wand to her. Annika pointed it at Wenlock and said, "For the love of my family and my people, I ask you to break all of Wenlock's spells." This time, because she used it out of love, not hate, the wand worked!

Wenlock aimed his wand at Annika. *Zap!* The evil magic and the good magic met in midair. The Wand of Light's power was so strong that it melted Wenlock's wand! All of a sudden, the griffin turned into a scrawny cat. The three trolls became the beautiful women they had once been.

Back at the village, the King, the Queen, and the villagers were no longer statues. The spell was broken!

Brietta, Aidan, and Annika quickly flew home on the two beautiful flying horses. When Annika arrived at the castle, the King and Queen were happy to have her back safe and sound.

"Are you ready for a surprise?" Annika asked them.

Their parents gasped as Brietta entered the room. "Impossible!" said the King. "I can't believe you're with us again."

"It was Annika," said Brietta. "She never gave up hope."

Annika, the princess who loved adventure, was glad to be back home. And now that she had a new sister and a new friend, she was sure there would be many more adventures to come!